D0876730

Erotic Jamaican Tales

K. Sean Harris

©2005 K. Sean Harris
First Edition 2005
10 9 8 7 6 5 4 3 2 1
Second Edition 2007
10 9 8 7 6 5 4 3 2
Reprint 2016
10 9 8 7 6 5 4 3

All rights reserved. No part of this book may be reproduced, stored in a retrieval system, or transmitted, in any form or by any means, electronic, mechanical, photocopying, recording, or otherwise, without the expressed written permission of the publisher or author.

This is a work of fiction. Names, characters, places and incidents either are the products of the author's imagination or are used fictitiously, and any resemblance to actual persons, living or dead, events or locales, is entirely coincidental.

Cover Design: Lee-Quee & Riley Limited
Typeset & Book layout: PAGE Services

Published by: Book Fetish

www.kseanharris.com

Printed in the U.S.A.   ISBN: 978-610-703-3

A DAY WITHOUT SEX IS A DAY WASTED.

Anonymous

ALSO BY K. SEAN HARRIS

Novels

The Snake Charmer
Detour
Queen of the Damned
Blood of Angels
Blood of Angels II
Kiss of Death
The Garrison
The Heart Collector
Death Incarnate
Merchants of Death
The Stud
The Stud II

Anthologies

The Sex Files
The Sex Files Vol. 2
More Erotic Jamaican Tales

Contents

The Stallion

THE STALLION

"*M*y god!" she exclaimed, as she gaped at his phallus. In her forty-five years she had seen her ample share of cocks but this was by far the biggest she had ever laid eyes upon. It was gargantuan. Her lips quivered as she wondered how much of it she could possibly get in her mouth.

She didn't have long to ponder. Conrad moved towards her purposefully, his dick waving like an iron flag. He stopped an inch from her. They gazed lustfully at each other, not touching. Her five inch stilettos allowing her to match his five-eleven frame. After eight seconds of thick sexual tension, Conrad placed both hands on her shoulders and gently directed her downwards.

She squatted instead of kneeling, her plump vulva gaping obscenely above the floor. She ran her hand along its length, thinking excitedly that it had to be at least a foot long. The tip was slick with pre-cum. Conrad moaned when her hot mouth enveloped the head of his dick. Jennifer placed her free hand on his rather bony thigh and warmed to the task at hand. She pumped his shaft slowly, expertly sucking his dick with a variety of techniques. Conrad groaned in ecstasy, grabbing a fistful of her mane as she swallowed him as deep as her mouth would allow.

Jennifer stopped sucking him when she felt his dick pulsing, knowing he was near orgasm.

"Slow down big boy," she cooed, "I'm not ready for you to cum just yet."

He helped her to her feet and they moved over to the tan leather couch next to the parrot cage.

Conrad glanced at the multi-coloured parrot and the bird seemed to wink at him. For some reason, the parrot made him uncomfortable. Jennifer, who had leaned over the arm of the couch, sensed his hesitation.

"What's wrong?" she asked, looking at him over her shoulder.

"Nutten, is jus' that the damn bird keep watching mi."

"Oh please. Ignore Mary; the stupid bird hasn't spoken a word since I bought her. Come over here and break me in two with that donkey dick of yours," she purred, wiggling her ass provocatively.

Conrad grinned as he took a condom from his pocket. They were both still fully clothed; his dick jutting from the fly of his jeans. Jennifer's short dress was hiked around her waist as she waited impatiently for him to penetrate her. Condom finally in place, Conrad held her by her hips and slowly guided his dick inside her. Jennifer gasped as her pussy stretched to accommodate him.

"Ohhh...good god! Hold on just a sec..." Jennifer croaked as she spread her legs wider and adjusted her torso.

"Ok, fill me up now big boy...give me every inch of that big black dick," she commanded. Conrad obliged, pushing his dick deep inside her. She groaned like a wounded animal as he slowly got into a rhythm. He felt her muscles contracting and grabbing his dick as he as began to quicken his pace.

"I feel it in my throat," Jennifer moaned, holding onto the couch for dear life as he pummeled her furiously.

"Slap my ass!" she instructed.

She squealed with pleasure as Conrad administered four generous slaps in quick succession to her right ass cheek. Jennifer reached down and furiously massaged her engorged clit as Conrad ravaged her pussy.

"Oh fuck...I'm coming Conrad!" she shouted, lost in the throes of the most intense orgasm she'd had in years. Jennifer bucked like a wild animal as her pussy showered his dick with its juices.

Conrad kept up his frantic pace; fucking her like his life depended on it. Jennifer moaned appreciatively, thinking she'd probably pass out if she came again. She was still reeling from the intensity of the first orgasm.

Her pussy throbbed as Conrad lifted one of her legs, his heavy balls slapping against the inside of her right thigh.

"Oh yes...that's it...fuck me Conrad!" Jennifer implored, making eye contact as Conrad bore in and out of her glistening cunt at what seemed like a hundred miles per hour. His T-shirt was soaked with perspiration. Conrad grunted as he felt himself nearing climax.

"I feel you coming..." Jennifer gasped between breaths, "I want you to come in my mouth."

This utterly wanton admission drove Conrad crazy. He pulled out of her pussy and franticly rolled off the condom. Jennifer quickly turned around and sank to her knees as Conrad emitted a guttural growl and erupted in her face. She closed her eyes as his hot juice splashed her face and hair. When the torrent ended, she opened her eyes and licked the remaining juices off his dick.

Conrad trembled, his nerves frayed by her wanton behavior. He had never met anyone like her.

"Damn Conrad, you just gave me the fuck of my life," Jennifer said, as she stood up, her face and hair glistening with his juices.

Conrad smiled contentedly as he sat on the arm of the couch, his dick hanging limply from his fly like an indecent snake.

"Well, that was superb but you've got to get going now. I have some work to do before I go to bed," Jennifer said, as she looked around for her pocketbook.

"After the ride you just gave me, I'll surely need all the rest I can get tonight. I'm not a spring chicken anymore you know," she added jokingly.

They both knew that she looked great and was in excellent shape for her age.

"So when mi can see yuh again?" Conrad asked, as he got up from the couch, fixing his clothes.

"I'll call you," Jennifer replied as she rummaged through her Burberry pocketbook. She took out three crisp one thousand dollar bills and handed the money to Conrad.

"Put this in your pocket," she said.

Conrad gazed at the money in her outstretched hand. It felt a little weird but that was what he made weekly, packing groceries at an uptown supermarket in Barbican. It would be stupid of him not to take it.

"Thanks," he mumbled, taking the money and stuffing it inside his pocket.

"Don't mention it," Jennifer replied, as she picked up the phone. Conrad watched her as she called her trusted cabbie to take him home. *Even with semen all over her she still looks classy*, he mused.

"Taxi will be here in five minutes," she announced. "Would you like something to drink in the meantime?"

"Yeah, a red stripe would be cool."

Jennifer returned from the kitchen and handed him a bottle of red stripe beer.

"Here you go, my stallion," she said.

"Thanks," Conrad replied, as the phone rang loudly. He looked at the parrot as Jennifer went into another room to take the call. The bird watched him with intelligent eyes. Conrad felt like opening the cage and choking the bird to death. A horn beeped twice outside.

Jennifer, still on the phone, returned to the living room and placed her hand over the mouthpiece. "I'll call you soon, bye big boy," she purred.

"Ok, see you," Conrad said as he went through the door. The night was starry and cool, and he felt great as he entered the cab, still sipping his beer.

"Where to?" asked the driver as Conrad closed the door.

"Jus' drop me down ah Grants Pen road," Conrad replied.

As the taxi sped off, Conrad reclined his seat and reminisced on the day he had met the attractive middle-aged woman. It was a week ago, Thursday evening, about half an hour before closing time. He was chatting with a couple co-workers. The supermarket was almost empty when she walked in. They all watched her as she selected a trolley and briskly strode towards the fresh produce aisle.

"Jah know, she look good fi a big woman," the fat one everyone called Fatta remarked.

"She look like she have money too," Benjy added.

Conrad tuned them out and walked over to where she was carefully examining a huge cucumber.

"Good evening, Ma'am. Yuh need any help loading your trolley?"

She looked at him before responding. "Sure, why not? Fetch me some tomatoes and some green peppers."

He hurried to do her bidding. The day had been slow and he could use a big tip. When she had gotten everything she needed, he pushed the trolley to the cashier. As she walked beside him, he could smell her perfume. It was an unfamiliar scent but it reminded him of roses. Her business suit was tailored to perfection, emphasizing her lush curves. He felt his cock stir in the confines of his tight jeans. The dress code at work was a white shirt tucked into blue or black jeans.

After she settled her bill, paying by credit card, they headed out to the parking lot. She directed him to a huge black SUV nestled between a smaller SUV and a BMW sports car. She opened the back and he loaded her bags into the luxurious vehicle. When he was through, she gave him a cool calculating gaze, which lingered a bit at the bulge in his crotch. She fished out her pocket book and gave him five hundred dollars; a very generous tip.

"Thank you very much, ma'am," Conrad said gratefully.

"You can thank me by calling me Jennifer. Ma'am makes me feel so old," she replied. "Do I look old young man?"

"Oh no ma'…I mean Jennifer," he stammered. "You look really good."

"Thank you," she said, smiling. "I was only teasing."

Then she suddenly leaned forward and grabbed his crotch. Conrad was so shocked he couldn't move. She seemed amused by the incredulous look on his face.

"Well, well…what have we got here? Do you have a permit to carry this thing around?" she asked with a laugh. "I hope you know how to use it properly…"

"Yes, Jennifer," he responded brightly, now that he was on sure footing.

"Good. Give me your number," she said, taking out her expensive cell phone.

Conrad gave her his name and number, still in awe at the unexpected turn of events.

"Ok, Conrad...I'll give you a call one of these days."

"Ok," he replied as she turned away and entered her vehicle.

"Which part a Grants Pen road yuh a come off youth?" the taxi driver asked, interrupting his thoughts. He looked out the window to get his bearings.

"Drop mi off at the square," he replied.

Two minutes later, Conrad was walking down the lane that led to the ramshackle two-bedroom house he shared with his grandmother.

"Big wood Conrad," a bow-legged browning named Stacey said as he turned the corner.

She was standing with two other girls, smoking a spliff.

"What a gwaan Stacey?" he replied, nodding a greeting to the other girls.

His exceptional dick size was common knowledge here in the ghetto of Grants Pen and its environs. He had fucked all three girls at one time or another.

"Nutten much. Come link me lata, mi feel fi a proper fix," she said, through a haze of weed smoke.

"Alright, cool. Lata then," Conrad said, as he continued home.

Meanwhile, Jennifer was in her marble tub, enjoying a bubble bath, her pussy pleasantly sore. It had been quite some time since she had gotten such a satisfying fuck. *That kid was something else*, she marveled, squeezing her nipples. That was a nice stroke of luck, her stopping by the supermarket on impulse. Normally, grocery shopping would have been done on a Saturday at her regular supermarket, closer to home.

The sound of the front door slamming broke into her thoughts. Her husband of fifteen years was home. He was a white American businessman who had fallen in love with Jamaica over twenty years ago and eventually became a dual citizen. He loved her and treated her well, but couldn't satisfy her sexual needs. But to be fair, she giggled to herself, few men could. She was a true nymph. She had to be careful though, Peter was a jealous man and had a licensed revolver. Conrad was the first man she took home to fuck. She usually went to one of the many motels scattered around Kingston.

"I'm home Jen," she heard him announce.

"I'm in the tub honey," she replied, adding, "Dinner's in the microwave."

Five minutes later, Jennifer strolled into the living room to find her potbellied husband reclining on the couch, with a drink in hand.

"Hey baby," he said, looking at her long legs.

Being in the living room made her remember what had taken place there a few hours earlier and she could feel her pussy getting wet. She dropped her towel in response.

Peter put his drink down on the mahogany coffee-table as his wife approached him. Every time he saw her naked body, he had to marvel at how attractive she still was after all these years.

Silent, she unbuckled his pants and eased them down to his ankles along with his underwear. Jennifer took her husband's pale, half-erect prick in her mouth, inhaling its scent, musky from a long day at the office. It wasn't nearly half as big as Conrad's, hell, not even a quarter. But it would have to suffice. She was in heat.

Peter moaned under his wife's oral attention. Jennifer licked and sucked his balls as she stroked his dick. When he was fully erect, she straddled him.

She rode him feverishly with visions of Conrad's anaconda embedded in her brain. She squeezed her nipples as Peter bucked upwards, trying to match her frantic pace.

Then a crazy thing occurred.

Mary, the parrot, fluttered in her cage, and screeched loudly and clearly, "Fuck me Conrad! Fuck me with that big black dick!"

The couple froze on the couch, staring in shock at the parrot that, before now, had never uttered a word.

8

The Night Crawler

NIGHT CRAWLER

"*How* much?" Nigel asked, through the halfway down window of his blue 2005 Honda CRV.

"Depends on what you want," the taller of the two women responded.

Nigel appraised the two prostitutes. The one who answered him was the more attractive of the two. She was tall, maybe five-ten. A bit on the skinny side but her breasts were huge, with large prominent nipples. She was cute, her exotic features suggesting a hint of Indian heritage. Ah boy, Jamaica was truly out of many one people. She looked at him questioningly through luminous brown eyes. She looked fresh, possibly had only been hooking for a couple of weeks.

Nigel prided himself on being quite the expert. He certainly qualified, having bought pussy all over Jamaica consistently for the past four years.

"So what yuh saying," the other whore prompted. She was thick, her voluptuous thighs stretching her red mini-skirt to capacity. She had a protruding stomach but overall not a bad body. Her face was too plain though. Nigel only went for the cute ones. As ugly as he was, he'd be damned if he spent good money on an ugly chick. During his childhood, if Nigel had a dollar for every time someone had teased him by asking 'if him escape from zoo', he'd be a multi-millionaire by now.

He gestured for the tall one to approach the vehicle. She strutted over to him as if she was modeling on a runway in Milan. He felt the beginning of an erection as she approached. Nigel put his window down a bit further.

"I want a blowjob and a fuck," he declared, getting straight to the point.

"Three thousand," she replied.

"No problem, where…?"

"Just drive down to where you see that big gate," she said, pointing to what, according to the brightly painted sign, was a wholesale enterprise. "The security guard will let you park inside for a hundred dollars."

Nigel drove the sixty or so meters and pulled up at the gate. The security guard opened up and Nigel handed him a hundred dollar bill, wondering idly how much money the guard pulled in nightly with this side hustle.

"Dim yuh light," the guard instructed, as Nigel drove in.

He could see why. There were about six vehicles parked on the premises. One girl was bent over the hood of a car getting it on doggy style, while a man, his car door open obstructing view of the prostitute, was standing by his car getting what appeared to be the blowjob of his life; if the loud animal-like sound he was emitting was anything to go by.

The others were inside their vehicles. The yellow pick-up truck over to the right was rocking like it was on hydraulics. Nigel switched off his engine and waited for the girl. She came to the window instead of coming inside the vehicle.

"Outside or in?" she queried, adding, "You have to pay first."

"I know the rules girl," Nigel snapped, slightly annoyed.

She stuffed the money in a tiny purse and put it in her knee-length boots. Nigel switched on the power in his CRV and put on a CD featuring the latest reggae hits. He opened the door and turned to face the prostitute. She loosened his jeans and Nigel freed one leg to give himself more leverage.

"So what's your name?" he asked idly, as she reached for his dick.

"Simone," she replied.

Yeah right, Nigel mused. He felt her hesitate for a second when she felt his cock. He wondered for perhaps what was the millionth time, if he was put here to suffer for the sins of his ancestors, for him to be so cursed. Not only did he closely resemble a baboon, but his dick had decided to stop growing when he turned thirteen.

That was the main reason he only fucked prostitutes. At least they wouldn't laugh in his face and he never had to see them again. His first attempt to have a girlfriend had failed miserably and he had taken an oath that he would only buy sex thereafter. Denise had been cruel, that bitch had traumatized him for life.

They sat beside each other in economics during his first semester and a friendship had blossomed fairly quickly. To this day, he never could figure out why she dated him, but grateful to finally have a girlfriend, he never asked. They dated for a month before she decided to get intimate with him.

On that unforgettable Friday night, they went to the cinema to check out an action-comedy. They had a great time and went back to campus to chill in her room on one of the three student dorms. They sat on her bed laughing about scenes in the movie when she began to kiss him. He had gotten so excited, clumsily returning her kisses in earnest; overwhelmed by the need to finally shed the weighty burden of his virginity. But, alas, it was not to be.

When Denise put her hand in his pants, she froze momentarily before screaming at the top of her voice, "Nigel! Weh yuh wood deh? How a big man buddy can so tiny?"

Someone walking by in the hallway erupted with laughter as Nigel's very black face flushed purple with embarrassment and shame. Nigel forced the distasteful memory aside as the prostitute bent over and began sucking his four inch erection. She deep throated him easily. Nigel freed her breasts from her halter top as she sucked his dick vigorously.

He groaned as she managed to get his entire genitalia in her mouth; balls and all. Nigel started to gyrate his waist to the beat of the reggae track playing. Not wanting to cum before sampling the pussy he paid for, he stopped her and rolled on a condom. He got out of the vehicle and bent her over doggy style, her hands using the seat and dashboard for balance.

She was silent when he entered her pussy, not quite sure if he was in yet. Two of the vehicles on the premises started up and quickly drove out. Nigel began pumping away like a jackrabbit.

"Talk to me girl," Nigel implored excitedly. "Tell mi how mi buddy sweet!"

She struggled to contain laughter.

"Yes big daddy…that feel real good," she said convincingly. *I should win an Actor Boy award (Jamaica's version of the Oscars) for this performance*, she mused.

"Yuh love it baby?" Nigel asked as he slapped her small bum, completely lost in his own world.

"Oh yes…don't stop," she said as she reached under to search for his balls. She eventually found them and gave them a slight squeeze, hoping it would help to push him over the brink. It worked.

Nigel's body convulsed as he ejaculated with a triumphant roar. Bright headlights suddenly shone on Nigel. A bit disoriented, he put up his hand to block out the light. Then he saw the blue lights flashing at the top of the car and his knees became weak.

It was the police.

The Discovery

THE DISCOVERY

I stared emptily at the dry landscape as sweat pooled between my voluptuous breasts. As usual, I was not looking directly at my husband as he expounded on the merits of investment banking. The sky was clear blue, the air humid and the dry brown shrubs waved in the wind as they crouched at the side of the road.

The limbs of the foliage seemed to do a curious dance as my husband drove faster in order to cool down the car. The air conditioner was broken. The car was a 1973 Mercedes sedan and had been passed down to him by his dad, so he stubbornly refused to buy a new car. The sun was beating down on my skin like pinpricks of fire and my husband of eight months was annoying me to death with his constant jabbering about the stock market and the gains he had made the previous week.

I glanced at him wearily and wondered if he had any idea that I was not interested in his latest financial conquest. He looked over at me and smiled, his face lighting up. "I'm not boring you, am I?" he asked.

"No, why would you think that?" I slightly bared my teeth in the semblance of a smile and turned my head to look back out the window.

"Something is wrong Bridgette, I can feel it." He pushed his glasses up his nose and slowed the car a bit. "Are you upset because we're going to visit my parents?"

"No Roger, I'm ok." I tried to control my voice and not flare up as I tended to do these days. Everything he said annoyed me. He was just so clueless and not for the first time, I castigated myself inwardly that I was not being fair to the friendly, caring man that I married.

"Bridgette, my parents like you, really." He looked at the time and sighed. "I'm sorry that my mother always seems to pick on you but I guess it's because she thinks that you're too young for me, but with time, it will pass."

I nodded and sighed. Mrs. Linton thought I was the worst thing that could ever happen to her beloved son. She took one look at me the Sunday morning that Roger had dragged me to meet his family and promptly decided that I was not suitable. My hair was wrong because I kept it short and closely cropped, my clothes were wrong because I didn't shop at the elegant boutiques that she frequented with her friends and my education was wrong because I wasn't college educated. She visibly shuddered when she heard her precious son met me in a shoe store where I worked as a clerk and had the audacity to want to marry me.

They were true Jamaican upper class: they had a beachfront villa in Negril, a yacht that they hosted parties on and the Linton name was synonymous with banking in Jamaica.

I was in awe of Roger when I found out that he was one of *The* Linton's and that he was interested in me. He obviously found me attractive and I was happy that my better than average breasts and my well rounded butt was always an eye catcher for men. I invited his attentions and gave him the fuck of his nerdy life on the fourth date; using every sexual trick that my freaky ex-boyfriend Paul had taught me, and then some, to ensure that I would not be forgotten.

I was eighteen at the time and Roger was approaching his twenty-eighth birthday. I was so immature and idealistic then; nobody told me that money and fame were not all. There wasn't a manual to tell me what to do after marrying a rich man you didn't love. Our sex life was going downhill fast and if I had to fake one more orgasm, I would just die.

I shifted uncomfortably on the car seat. More and more, I was dreaming of Paul and how sexy and spontaneous he was. I'd been fucked in the bathroom at a fast food restaurant, masturbated to an orgasm at the movies, impaled sitting on his lap at a table at the Asylum nightclub…god, let me stop before I drench the car seat. My flimsy little g-string wouldn't be able to absorb much moisture.

We drew up at the Linton estate in Mandeville, after driving in relative silence for much of the journey. The air felt lighter and I inhaled deeply as I stepped out of the car. The vast house stood overlooking the town and the rolling hills in the distance.

"Uncle Roger!" squealed a little boy in blue as he came running down the steps to greet his doting uncle. "I missed you," he said, his little face scrunched up in consternation as he viewed his uncle.

"I missed you too." Roger grabbed his nephew and hugged him tight. "You're not going to say hello to your Auntie Bridgette?"

The little boy looked over at me and whispered, "Hi Auntie Bridgette."

"Hi TJ." I smiled, knowing it was not genuine. The child was the first grandchild of the Linton's and was spoiled rotten by all around him. He was disruptive and loud and I think I slightly hated him. Here goes the next three days of noise and mayhem. I sighed and grabbed the bag that had my belongings.

"Oh, Bridgette," Mrs. Linton said, as I entered the house. "I had no idea that you were coming," she added, lying through her teeth. She made the cursory glance at my sexy shorts and skimpy top and sighed. "As usual, you look positively indecent."

"Hello to you too, Tabitha." I smiled as she gritted her teeth. She hated when I called her by her first name. But what could I do, her other daughters-in-law called her mom and she made it quite clear I was not to even think about it.

"Hello Bridgette." He stood quietly in the doorway, his tall muscular frame encased in a grey sweater and slacks.

I jumped nervously.

"Hello Thomas," I said softly. Roger's father always made me feel nervous. He was not snobbish like his wife or unwelcoming, but I was always disquieted by his presence. I ran my fingers through my short hair, knowing that the curls would stand on end, but I had to do something with my hands. My heart raced as he watched me. I licked my parched lips and he cleared his throat.

"Well it is good to see you; I have not seen you since Christmas. I thought you would have come for my birthday," he said, faintly accusing.

"Well she didn't," Tabitha jumped in, "and I for one did not miss her." She gave me a hostile look and flounced off to greet her son who was still in the driveway answering his nephew's questions.

"Do you need help with the bag?" Thomas asked.

"No…I think I can manage…" I stammered, feeling hot and bothered though the Mandeville breeze was cool.

He stood in front of me and silently stared. "I'll take it anyway," he said after what seemed like a long time.

I had no choice but to follow him silently up the long, circular stairs as he headed for the room that was always assigned to his son when he came to stay.

I watched his broad back and swallowed convulsively. He was in his early fifties and still remarkably fit as he worked out frequently in his private gym. His face was distinguished looking and strong. When he smiled, his chocolate brown eyes lighted up and his face became animated, but when he was serious he was a force to be reckoned with. With one look, he could shut his wife up and quell her incessant bickering.

He was sexy and strong, and deep down I knew why I was always nervous and reluctant to visit. I could handle Tabitha with her snobbery, but I was afraid of the feelings that her husband invoked in me.

I was sexually attracted to my husband's father and he figured in most of my fantasies. When Roger would labour inside me, his body slick with sweat, I would close my eyes and think of his hunk of a father who was never far from my thoughts.

We reached the room and I was breathing heavily. there was an ache between my legs that would not go away.

"Here you are," he said, putting the bag on the floor.

He turned to the bed to check that everything was alright and then spun around to face me.

"You're breathing rather hard," he chuckled. "It is hard to believe that with a body like yours, you're not constantly at the gym." His eyes were glazed with open lust.

Silence reigned.

The sexual tension in the room was thicker than molasses. I found it difficult to breathe.

He moved closer to me and touched my nipples, which were growing harder by the minute.

"Is this for me, Bridgette?" he whispered, as he rubbed his fingers across them slowly. I gasped and slightly swayed toward him.

He emitted a low growl and lifted my blouse. I was braless and helpless to stop this welcome assault on my body.

He stared worshipfully at my full breasts. The nipples were rock hard and they felt oh so sensitive. He lowered his head and began to suck them. The cold wetness of his tongue was like fire set to a dry bush. My head was slightly spinning and my clit was throbbing unbearably. He was taking little nips from my breast and paying equal attention to both. I wanted him there and now. I wanted him to fuck me mercilessly on the floor.

I dazedly heard footsteps, and he must have heard them too because he pulled back and dragged down my blouse.

He looked tortured. "I want you so badly," he said earnestly. "I've wanted you from the first moment my son brought you home." He spun around and left me in the center of the room, horny and trembling.

It was harder than usual at dinner that evening. Thomas was sitting at the head of the table; I avoided looking at him. His other two sons, Devon and Damon, the twins, as their mother fondly referred to them, came with their wives.

As usual, I was treated as if I was the lowest of the low by the women. Heading the pack of course was Tabitha, the mother-in-law from hell.

Roger was very attentive to me and for a moment I felt bad, knowing what I had done with his father in the room that we were going to share later. The feeling of guilt quickly passed.

"Are you coming Bridgette?" Carmen, the first daughter-in-law asked me.

"Oh, sorry," I said, confused. "Where to...?"

"To the mayor's cocktail party," Tricia, the other one, supplied, looking at me as if I was mentally challenged.

"When is it?" I asked.

"Tonight," Tabitha said bitingly. "You might as well say no, because if that little mini-dress that you have on is any indication of what you're planning to wear, you won't be appropriately dressed."

Normally I would reply with spirit, but I was too out of it to care.

I shrugged.

"Don't mind mother," Roger said, playing his usual role as buffer. "I want you there darling. I have to give a speech; I donated some supplies to the basic school he patronizes."

Before I could reply, Thomas jumped in. "I have some urgent business to wrap up before I can make it." He looked at his wife and she remained silent.

"How long will the function take?" I asked Roger, suddenly interested in the details.

"Probably until midnight," Roger sighed, "and knowing mom, she is going to talk to the mayor's wife about god only knows what till the last person leaves."

"I'm a bit tired dear, I think I'll pass," I said to Roger, giving him what I hoped looked like a tired smile.

After much argument on Roger's part, he agreed for me to stay and twenty minutes later they all left, leaving Thomas and I alone in the house.

I was alone in the den trying to watch the television, struggling to drag my mind off the carnal. Where was Thomas? What was he doing?

As if I conjured him up from my mind, he came into the the room and sat on the sofa opposite mine.

The tension was back.

"Bridgette," he started; his voice low and husky, "I have wanted you since I first saw you."

I looked at him and sighed. "I feel it too. I can't deny there is this insane attraction."

He nodded gravely. "I don't want to hurt my son Bridgette; I know he loves you."

I watched tongue-tied as he loosened his tie. My throat was dry. The thong that I had on under my little dress was soaking wet.

I opened my legs a little; I was hot all over.

"Bridgette…" he whispered, "Don't look at me like that. I'm trying to hold it together and you're not making it easy for me." I fled the room. This was madness. I was caught up in a crazy situation. I went to the poolside and stripped to my thong and matching bra. I needed to cool off or probably just run away.

A hand touched my shoulder. I shuddered and turned my head, my legs quivering.

"Let's go inside the pool house," he said softly, looking defeated.

The pool house had a bed in the corner of the self-contained flat. He started to remove his clothing, piece by piece as he stared at me; daring me to back away.

His body was remarkable for a man of any age much less one in his early fifties. His cock sprang forth like an angry cobra when he removed his underwear. His cock was thick like a mayonnaise jar; veins prominent and bulging. It was a monster; its tip was red and the mushroom head big. Roger definitely was not built like his dad.

I swallowed.

He took me in his arms, his erection straining against my belly. He kissed me tentatively at first, then with rough passion.

His huge hands glided over my supple body, tweaking my nipples and cupping my freshly shaven mound.

"You're so wet…" he breathed, as he tugged my thong across my clit.

"Thomas…please…"

"Please…what…"

"Please fuck me. I can't take it anymore!"

He pushed aside the flimsy thong and rammed his thick cock in my tight depths. It was as if he had come home. My muscles pulsed around him and I groaned his name.

"I can't believe I'm finally inside you," Thomas said as he administered long, deep strokes to my mid-section.

He felt strong and powerful as I wrapped my legs around him.

"Oh god...yes," I moaned, "Harder, deeper.... fuck...yeah."
He complied, plowing into me with wild abandon. I couldn't
take it any longer, the sweet ache in my pussy was building up
to a strong crescendo and I bit my lips as my body vibrated to
my first orgasm since I got married eight months ago.
"Yesss..!" I screamed, as I dug my nails into his muscular
back.
I marveled at his strength and stamina as he continued to
fuck me at a torrid pace. Thomas lifted me from against the wall
like a rag doll. Standing in the middle of the room, he impaled
me mercilessly. I felt like I was going to faint from ecstasy.
Why couldn't Roger make me feel like this?
Still deeply buried inside me, Thomas moved us over
towards the bed. He laid me on my back and placed my feet on
his shoulder. I swore I felt his dick in my belly.
"That's it Thomas!" I cried. "I'm cumming again!"
Thomas held my ankles and spread my legs as far as they
could possibly go. My eyes rolled to the back of my head as my
second orgasm in the past fifteen minutes rocked me to the core.
Thomas pulled out of my pussy at the last possible moment
and spewed hot semen all over my breasts and stomach.
"Oh Thomas...I can't move," I breathed, "That was incredible."
"It sure was," Thomas agreed, as he sat down on the bed.
I used a finger to scoop up a tiny bit of his semen off my
breast and licked my finger seductively.
"Oh you naughty girl," Thomas said, looking at me with
renewed passion. "I'd better go clean up before I jump you again."
He stood and stretched his muscular frame. "Besides, I
promised to show up at the mayor's cocktail reception."
"Yeah, you should get going."
Twenty minutes later, Thomas resurfaced at the pool house,
looking resplendent in a black blazer and Gucci loafers. I was
lying on the bed where he left me; legs widely spread with my
plump, hairless crotch on full display.
"Now that's a sight for sore eyes," Thomas murmured
appreciatively, standing by the doorway. I smiled, looking like
a porn star with all that semen on my body.

"You look great," I purred.

"I feel great, thanks to you."

I blew him a kiss.

"See you later sexy, I'm off," Thomas said, as he turned and left, but not before stealing another glance at the fat, juicy pussy on display.

Ten minutes had passed since I had heard the roar of Thomas' Chevy Avalanche going down the hill. With a sigh, I rose, gathered my clothes and went to the main house.

I took a nice hot shower and slipped into a sweater and yoga pants. Mandeville gets really chilly at night, especially on the hills. I put the radio on Irie FM and fell asleep to the sound of old reggae jams.

I awakened to find my husband gently shaking me.

"Morning darling; you must have been really tired last night," Roger said, "It's ten o' clock."

"Really," I yawned, "What time are we leaving for Kingston?"

"About two," Roger replied, "Are you hungry?"

"Starving; I want breakfast in bed sweetheart." I rubbed his crotch. "Pretty please?"

"Mother won't be pleased but ok. I'll be back in a bit."

I was sitting up in bed, enjoying the view when Roger returned with a tray.

"Thank you baby," I gushed, and dug into the ackee and saltfish and fried dumplings with gusto.

"I'll be down by the pool. Everyone is heading down there now."

"Ok hun," I mumbled, thoroughly enjoying my breakfast.

I didn't see Thomas before we left for Kingston. He was President of the Mandeville chapter of the Rifle Club and they were hosting an afternoon brunch at the Ridgeline Hotel and Spa.

It was a good ride back to Kingston. The afternoon was cool and the traffic was light. We had also stopped at the coconut man at the top of the Winston Jones highway and had a refreshing drink of coconut water.

Within two hours, we were pulling into our apartment complex on Lady Musgrave Drive. The two-bedroom apartment was lovely. As much as I disliked my mother-in-law, the witch had impeccable taste; she had furnished and decorated the apartment as a wedding gift to her favourite son, even though she hated his wife.

Wonder what the old biddy would do if she found out that I had slept with her sexy husband, I mused, the thought giving me a sense of satisfaction.

I was home alone the following day, preparing for my three o' clock class when the phone rang.

"Hello?"

"I can't stop thinking about you Bridgette. You're deep under my skin."

"Oh Thomas…what are we going to do?" I asked, leaning against the bedroom wall.

"I'm in Kingston, had some business to take care of. What's your schedule like today?"

"I only have one class today, at three." I was pursuing a first degree in Marketing; Roger had insisted I go back to school when we got married.

"Do you have to go? I really need to see you before I head back to Mandeville this evening."

"No, I can get the notes from my friend Nicole," I replied quickly.

"Great, I'll be there in half an hour," Thomas said happily and hung up.

I hurried excitedly to the bathroom to take a quick shower. The phone rang as I was rummaging through my lingerie drawer.

"Hello?"

"Babe, it's me. Have you seen a brown file labeled confidential?" Roger asked. "I think I might have left it on the kitchen counter this morning."

"No darling, I haven't seen it," I replied as I applied a splash of Dolce & Gabbana Feminine to my neck and breasts.

"Shit!" Roger exclaimed irritably. "I need it for a meeting this afternoon."

"I guess it must be here at the office somewhere," he went on, "You getting ready for class?"

"Yes darling," I said sweetly as I selected a sheer, red negligee to put on.

"Ok baby, see you later."

"Bye hun."

Thomas arrived ten minutes later. My pussy was moist as I opened the door to let him in. He took one look at my lush curves teasing him through the sheer material and lost all semblance of control.

He pulled me roughly to him and kissed me passionately, groping my ass crudely as I returned his kisses with equal ardor.

I helped him undress quickly, anxious to have him inside my tight orifice. We tumbled to the lush carpet and Thomas entered my pussy in one fluid motion. I held my ankles behind my ears as he plunged deeply into my warmth.

"Oh god I missed you," Thomas murmured as he continued to explore my depths.

"I missed you too Thomas," I cooed, "I miss the way you stretch my pussy to the limit."

I was now astride Thomas; riding him slowly and methodically. My slow, sensuous grinding was driving Thomas crazy. I milked his dick as I held his hands to my ample breasts. I suddenly increased the tempo, impaling myself on his rigid cock with all my might. I bounced up and down furiously, riding the wave towards my second climax of the afternoon.

Thomas slapped my ass with his huge hands, urging me to go faster. My breasts bounced sexily as I whimpered, begged and squealed myself to climax.

I got on my hands and knees and Thomas shafted me from behind, massaging my round butt as he felt himself nearing climax.

Bright sunlight suddenly flooded the living room as the front door flew open.

"Oh my god..." came the tortured cry from Roger as the unbelievable sight of his father's cock buried deeply into his moaning wife filled his eyes.

Thomas and I gaped at Roger stupidly. Gripped by the excitement of an unexpected afternoon romp with Thomas, I had totally overlooked the possibility of Roger coming home to look for the file.

What was going to happen now?

Dear Angie

DEAR ANGIE

 ear Angie,

Hi girl. Hope you're coping alright with the freezing London weather.

You won't believe what the fuck happened to me!

It was a Saturday night and my best friend Tori was celebrating her twentieth birthday. She had recently kicked her boyfriend to the curb (he didn't want to eat her pussy), so we decided to call up Monica and make it a girls' night out.

The Quad, Jamaica's only multi-level nightclub was packed but not to capacity. At first, we were in the Oxygen room but the DJ was playing too much house music so we went up to the Voodoo lounge. It was jumping in there. The latest reggae tunes were blasting and the dance floor was filled with gyrating couples and single women.

We were the epitome of sexy as we stood there talking and rocking to the music.

Then he came over.

He had been so confident and sure of himself when he approached me and offered to buy my friends and I a drink. He was nattily dressed in a nice striped Prada shirt, the club lights bouncing off his diamond encrusted necklace. He smelled great, just the right amount of cologne; you didn't smell him before you saw him.

Smooth. He was a real smooth guy.

"Hi there," he said to me, over the din of the music.

"Hey," I responded, checking him out and liking what I saw.

"I'm Jay," he offered, extending his hand.

"I'm Anika," I responded, shaking his hand, "and these are my friends Monica and Tori."

"So can I buy you ladies a drink?" Not waiting for a response, he gestured to a group of guys standing close by the bar and one of them picked up one of the three ice buckets resting on the bar and brought it over along with four glasses.

I was impressed.

He was a take charge kinda guy and I liked that. It didn't hurt that he was fine and had money too.

Jay filled our glasses with Moet and we toasted to Tori's birthday.

"You look really hot in that outfit," he whispered, his breath delightfully hot on my ear.

"Thank you," I purred. I was wearing a baby blue Armani off the shoulder top that emphasized my full breasts and cute white Capri pants that fitted my curvy body to perfection.

"So what do you do?" I asked, wanting to know more about the man I'd already decided to fuck tonight.

"I'm a businessman," he responded vaguely. A guy dressed in full white came over and whispered in Jay's ear. Jay said that he'd be back in a few and stepped off hurriedly.

"So what you guys think?" I asked my friends.

"Him look real good Anika," Tori enthused, adding, "I'll take him if you don't want him!"

We all laughed at that.

"He looks like a drug dealer," Monica muttered. "Did you see his necklace? Damn!"

Our favourite dancehall song came on and we all started to dance with gusto. I suddenly felt someone behind me and I turned my head, ready to curse. Jay had returned. He smiled and pulled me towards him. I didn't resist.

I settled into his arms and started gyrating slowly to the music. I expertly 'wined' my perky ass against him and I felt his erection salute my ass in appreciation. Jay rested a hand on my left thigh, caressing it as we moved as one, his erection feeling more powerful as I moved my waistline like a seasoned go-go dancer.

"Do you feel what you're doing to me?" he asked, biting me gently on my ear.

I shuddered.

I ground my ass against him more forcefully and he groaned in my ear.

The DJ turned the beat around and started playing some R&B. Jay sent for another bottle of Moet and poured us another round. This time, we danced face to face, crotch to crotch. He looked lustfully in my eyes as his fingers blazed a tantalizing trail down my back to my ass crack.

His hands were soft, very soft for a guy.

He cupped my ass as we rocked to the sound of Sade. Jay brushed his lips lightly against my neck and flicked his tongue against my ear.

"Be careful, that's my spot," I murmured huskily.

He chuckled and pinched my butt.

Two hours and eight glasses of Moet later, Jay rounded up his crew and we all went outside. The night air was cool and I was feeling horny and tipsy.

Tori was drunk, but insisted she wasn't through celebrating yet. Monica on the other hand, was ready to pack it in; said she had to get some sleep as she had to take her sister to the airport in a couple of hours.

Jay's pearl white, Lincoln Navigator was parked directly in front of the club and the black Ford F1-50 his crew traveled in was right behind it.

I could feel Jay's eyes on my ass as Tori and I walked Monica to her car. When she took off and we went back, Jay was in his truck, ready to go. I got in the front and Tori hopped in the back.

Jay turned on the DVD player and the image of a black man having sex with two Asian girls filled the screen.

"Now that's what I'm talking about!" Tori exclaimed, as the guy started to lick one of the girls' pussy. Jay chuckled and turned up the volume a bit.

We were driving along Constant Spring road when I noticed that Jay kept looking in the rear view mirror. Curious as to what was distracting him, I turned around. Tori's already short skirt was hiked up around her waist and she was masturbating. She didn't wear panties and neither did I. I bit my lips and involuntarily cupped my breasts as I watched the show Tori was putting on.

She had two fingers in her pussy as she massaged her humongous clit. We always teased her that her clit resembled a small dick. She started fingering herself rapidly, obviously nearing orgasm. Jay licked his lips and squirmed in his seat as Tori squealed from the back seat.

"Whew!" she exclaimed. "That was a nice appetizer," meeting Jay's eyes in the rear view mirror. I turned around and settled back in my seat. It was going to be an interesting end to tonight, I mused, my pussy throbbing in agreement.

We arrived at Jay's house about thirty minutes after leaving the club. It was a nice three-bedroom townhouse in Jacks Hill, an upscale residential area. The living room was sparsely but luxuriously furnished. A huge Plasma flat screen TV on a section of the wall, a black leather couch set, plush white carpeting and two large erotic sculptures dominated the room.

"The Jacuzzi is out on the patio ladies, make yourselves comfortable while I go get some champagne," Jay announced, as he sauntered off.

Tori eagerly led the way to the patio, undressing as she walked. I admired the huge tattoo above her ass crack; so sexy. I've always wanted one but I'm scared of needles. I glanced at my watch; it was four in the morning.

I watched Tori climb into the Jacuzzi as I slid out of my Capri pants. I pulled off my top and went to join my best friend; my body tingling with anticipation. We had fucked each other on several occasions, but had never fucked a guy together.

The Jacuzzi was still heating up when I stepped in. Tori immediately pulled me to her and invaded my mouth with her nimble tongue. We moaned as our tongues danced with each other.

"I see the fun has started without me," Jay grinned, holding a chilled bottle of Moet, a huge towel and a pack of condoms in his hands; his shiny black dick pointing at us.

He poured champagne on us as I sucked Tori's nipples and caressed her plump mound. It felt so erotic with the steam coming out the Jacuzzi and the champagne running down my body.

Tori and I parted as Jay eased into the middle. I kissed him passionately as Tori nibbled and caressed his chest. He moaned and placed the bottle of champagne on the edge of the Jacuzzi. Jay grabbed a fistful of my hair and bit my neck as he rubbed Tori's breasts with his free hand. Jay eased up out the water and sat on the edge. I bent down and licked the tip of his dick slowly, running my tongue around the rim as Tori took one his balls in her mouth. Jay closed his eyes as he enjoyed the incredible sensation of having two hot mouths on his genitals.

Tori moved behind me and I spread my legs expectantly as I tried to deep throat Jay's dick. I almost choked on it when Tori's tongue invaded my soaking wet pussy. I groaned loudly as she spread my ass cheeks, deliciously exposing my pussy and anus. She tongue-fucked my quivering pussy with gusto. I moaned in ecstasy as I pumped Jay's dick with my hand, unable to concentrate on sucking him while Tori continued her oral assault on my pussy.

Jay pinched my nipples and massaged my breasts as Tori ran her tongue up the crack of my ass while rubbing my clit. I almost fainted with pleasure. I changed position and sat on the edge of the Jacuzzi to allow Tori better access to my clit. Jay rolled on a condom and moved behind Tori. She gasped as Jay entered her. He fucked her slowly as she resumed eating my pussy. I maintained eye contact with Jay as I cupped my voluptuous breasts and sucked my nipples.

Tori started concentrating on my clit, nibbling and biting gently, then sucking on it passionately. "Oh Tori don't stop that…" I begged, as I felt my orgasm approaching. I threw my head back and roughly squeezed my nipples as I came in Tori's mouth.

My orgasm excited Jay and he began to fuck Tori hard and fast, grunting with each stroke. The water splashed noisily as Tori screamed for him to break his dick off inside her. I wondered idly if we had woken up the neighbors.

Jay stopped so we could switch positions. Tori sat on the edge with her legs widely spread. I licked her pussy like an ice cream cone as Jay fucked me doggy style at a slow pace. Tori pulled my hair painfully as I sucked her clit.

"Bumboclaat Anika!" Tori shouted obscenely, overcome with the intensity of her climax.

Jay took a swig from the bottle of champagne and placed me on the edge of the Jacuzzi. I threw one leg on his shoulder as he rammed his dick into my welcoming pussy. Tori played with my breasts and drank champagne while Jay fucked me like I had stolen money from him.

A blinking red light at the top left hand corner of the wall caught my eye but I dismissed it as probably being some kind of alarm.

"Fuck her pussy Jay," Tori coaxed, "dig out her belly."

Jay grunted loudly, unable to hold out any longer. He erupted like a volcano, quivering and trembling as Tori gently massaged his balls.

"Damn!" Jay said, rolling off the condom. "Pass the champagne!"

We laughed as he took a long swig. All three of us used the huge towel to dry ourselves and then we went to Jay's bedroom. We jumped onto the king size bed, Jay in the middle with Tori and I snuggled up contentedly on either side of him. I fell asleep with a smile on my face.

I woke up feeling groggy. Tori was still asleep, the sheet pulled down exposing her breasts. I looked at the clock on the dresser. It was twelve midday.

"Jah know, Jay" a voice said from the living room, "yuh nuh easy at all."

"The brown one have a fat pussy yo. Look pon har clit how it big!" another voice exclaimed.

"For real," a female agreed.

Who the rass are these people? What the hell are they looking at?

I got up and looked in Jay's closet for a shirt to put on. I slipped on a long sleeved Moschino shirt and buttoned two of the buttons as I went out to the living room.

I stopped dead in my tracks.

Five men, including Jay, and two girls, were scattered about the living room eating pizza and watching yours truly on the big screen plasma TV, getting fucked by Jay as I greedily ate Tori's pussy.

"Jay!" I screamed furiously, "You fucking pussyhole!"

Shit. I'll have to write the rest later Angie. Someone's at the door.

Lucky Day

LUCKY DAY

"*G*oal! Goal!" The national stadium erupted in bedlam, reacting to the crafty goal scored by star forward Orane Jones, putting Jamaica up by one. It was a must win game for Jamaica if they hoped to qualify for the World Cup. The Reggae Boyz, as the team was affectionately known worldwide, was five minutes away from victory - if they could just hold off the desperate Mexicans.

The national stadium was a sea of yellow and green, the dominant colours of the team. Almost everyone was standing, cheering and willing the national football team to victory. The cheers rained down from the stands as the referee blew the final whistle, signaling the end of the game. Jamaica was on its way to Germany next year; the only Caribbean team to qualify for the World Cup finals.

Duane and Ricky, his long-time friend visiting from New Jersey, hurried out to the parking lot, hoping to get a head start before the majority of the celebratory crowd started to leave. A group of four girls, a few meters ahead of them, had the same idea. The one on the extreme right with the long hair twisted loosely into a pony-tail caught Duane's eye. Her ass was big and round. It was if she had two soccer balls stuffed in the back of her skin-tight hipster jeans.

"Ricky, yuh see that?" Duane asked, pointing at the girl excitedly.

"Yeah son, shorty got a fatty," Ricky replied, spewing hip hop slang in an American accent. The two had been neighbours for years, before Ricky's family had migrated to the US some twelve years ago. The two friends stayed close and Duane had stayed at Ricky's home on numerous occasions.

The girls, laughing and chatting, entered the vast parking lot and veered right. Fortunately, Duane's ultra-fast Evolution VII was parked in the same direction. Ricky stopped by the car and Duane tossed him the keys and continued following the girls.

They stopped next to a red sedan about fifty meters away his car.

"Excuse me," Duane said, as he caught up to the girls. They all looked at him questioningly.

"Hi, can I talk to you for a minute?" he queried, looking directly at the object of his lust.

She approached him slowly, a sly smile playing at the corners of her luscious lips.

The other girls snickered at a comment one of them made.

"What's up Mr. Big Driver?" she said coolly.

Duane chuckled, realizing that she had recognized him. Duane was a local celebrity in the race car circuit. He was currently ranked the number one race car driver in Jamaica.

"Didn't figure you for a racing fan," Duane said, as he admired her sexy curves.

"Yeah man! I really love it! I rarely miss a meet," she gushed, adding, "your last race was really something."

Race car driving was getting popular in Jamaica and the meets were always well attended and exciting. The race she was referring to had catapulted Duane to the number one ranking after he had beaten Cory Pierce in the final.

"The name's Duane, but call me D," he said, extending his hand.

She shook it, responding, "Nice to meet you D, I'm Keisha."

Keisha had noticed Duane for some time, his skill behind the wheel excited her and he was really cute. She wasn't shy by any means, and would have approached him a long time ago if her jealous, possessive ass of a boyfriend wasn't always there with her. This was one of the rare occasions she got a chance to hang out with her girlfriends without him tagging along. Fortunately, he was off the island for three days.

Funny meeting him here, she mused. It must be fate.

"So can I have your number Keisha?" Duane asked, whipping out his cell phone expectantly, ready to store it.

"Keisha! Hurry up nuh!" her friend with the dreadlocks shouted. "I don't want to get stuck in the traffic."

"In a minute," Keisha replied, waving her off.

"No, you can't have my number," Keisha said to him, watching as disappointment blanketed his cute face. "But I'll take yours," she added, smiling.

Duane smiled back and happily gave her his digits. She stored the number in her cell phone and promised to call him later that night. Duane watched as she went into the waiting car. She was by far one of the sexiest girls he had ever seen. Often times when a woman had such a huge ass, she didn't have the breasts to go along with it. Keisha had the complete package.

I have to fuck her, Duane thought as he walked to his car. Ricky was sitting in the passenger seat with the door open, bopping his head to the hip hop beat blaring from the speakers. He turned down the music as Duane got behind the wheel.

"You got the digits?" he asked as the car pulled off into the traffic streaming out to the main road.

"Yeah man! Yuh dun know I'm the girl's dem suga," Duane replied, laughing.

"Whatever man," Ricky said, grinning.

"Keisha, I hope you're not thinking about calling him, girl," her opinionated friend Sharon intoned. "You know how jealous and crazy Winston is."

"Winston bumbo," Keisha declared, and they all laughed at her response.

Roughly seventy minutes later, Keisha was home at her apartment in Mona, taking a shower. *I only have two days before Winston returns from his trip so I have to move fast*, Keisha mused, making up her mind to invite Duane over that very night.

Her cell phone rang from where she had placed it on the toilet seat. She opened the shower curtain and answered it.

"Hello."

"What a gwaan babes?" Winston's deep baritone asked, as Keisha rolled her eyes.

"Hey you," Keisha replied, trying to keep the note of irritation out of her voice. He had called three times during the football match, where she couldn't even hear him because of the noise, twice during the ride home and here he was, calling yet again.

"What yuh up to?" he asked.

Getting ready to give away your pussy, she wanted to tell him. Instead she replied,"I'm taking a shower; just got in."

"Alright baby, mi will call you back lata," he responded.

"Later Winston."

"I miss you," Winston said, but Keisha had already hung up. *Rass man*! Keisha fumed, ruing the day she got involved with him. But how was she to know beforehand how insanely jealous he was? Giving a woman space was a foreign concept to Winston. She would have called it quits a long time ago but she was actually scared of him. Winston had a very bad temper, a licensed firearm and a politician father with wide connections. A man like that might think he can do anything and get away with it.

Keisha sighed and dried her voluptuous body, looking at herself in the full length mirror. She knew she was devastatingly sexy. Men were forever coming on to her or giving her lustful looks and admiring glances. The attention drove Winston crazy. She went into the bedroom and lathered herself with her favourite moisturizer. She wondered what Duane was doing and decided to call him after she had something to eat.

Duane and Ricky were seated at the bar of one of Kingston's trendy sports bars having a few drinks. He took a sip of his Guiness and lit a cigarette as Ricky tried to run game on a sweet looking dark complexioned girl who was getting a drink at the bar. He watched them idly as he thought about Keisha. It amazed him how much she had gotten under his skin. One brief meeting, and here he was, feeling like a love-struck, lust filled schoolboy and not the popular race car stud that he was.

"Yo D," Ricky said, interrupting his thoughts. "This is Carmen."

I waved hi.

"We're going over to a booth to kick it for awhile, aiight," he announced, American accent in full swing.

They sauntered off to a corner booth and waved over a waitress. Keisha, having eaten and was know sipping on a light beer, picked up the phone to call Duane. It rang in her hand. It was Winston, of course. She told him she was going to lie down for a bit as her head was hurting from all the noise and excitement at the football game earlier. He hung up promising to check up on her later that night.

Duane was talking to some people he knew when his cell phone vibrated in his pocket.

"Hello?"

"Hi D. Its Keisha."

"Hi sexy, what's up?" Duane said, trying not to sound too excited.

"I want to see you, now," she purred seductively.

Oh yes, there is a God, Duane thought happily. "Give me your address."

She gave him directions and he hurried over to Ricky, who was in deep conversation with his new friend.

"Ricky, mi haffi make a move," Duane said, grinning.

Ricky gave him a pound, smiling. "Handle your biz son."

Duane gave him the key to the apartment and left.

He drove like he was at one of his track meets, reaching Keisha's apartment in record time. He parked and knocked at her door.

Keisha opened the door and smiled at him invitingly.

"You plan on coming in or you're just going to stand there and fuck me with your eyes?"

Duane was rooted at the doorway gaping at Keisha's curves, currently spilling out of a batty-rider shorts and a tank top. He growled and stepped towards her, slamming the door behind him. Keisha stepped backwards, backing towards the bedroom. He continued walking towards her, his cock making a tent of his crotch. He reached her and kissed her juicy lips forcefully. She cupped the back of his head with one hand and held his dick with the other as they backed slowly into the bedroom.

She raised her hands as he pulled off her top. Her luscious breasts tumbled free. Duane bent his head and sucked her right nipple while he groped her ass cheeks, marveling at their size and firmness.

He trailed kisses down her flat stomach, passing to tug her navel ring gently with his teeth. Keisha groaned and pushed him on the bed. She unbuckled his jeans and removed it along with his boxers in one swift motion.

He moaned and ran his fingers through her hair as she licked the insides of his thighs alternately, slowly working her way up to his scrotum. He whimpered and crawled up on the bed when she blew on his genitals, taking her time, teasing him. She sucked his balls, singly, then together, twirling them around in her mouth.

Duane didn't think he could take much more. By the time her generous mouth covered his dick, his body was a mass of quivering flesh. He had never felt like this before. She was really putting it on him.

She ran her lips along the side of his shaft, squeezing the head and licked away the bit of pre-cum that had oozed out; sticking her tongue in the slit. Duane crawled further up the bed, begging her to stop.

She didn't.

She crawled with him, sucking, until his back was against the bed-head, unable to go any further. She sucked his dick vigorously, enjoying the power she had over him.

"Lawd….jesus…" Duane moaned, grabbing her hair. "Ah can't tek it nuh more."

His balls tightened and his dick pulsed as he started to buck in her mouth, she opened wide and allowed him to thrust in and out, cupping his balls and grinding them softly together.

Duane squealed like a bitch as he came; shooting his hot semen down Keisha's willing throat. She swallowed every drop.

"Oh my god…" Duane said softly. "Dat is the best blowjob mi eva get."

Keisha smiled wickedly and got up and went to the bathroom, her tremendous ass bouncing with each step.

Duane sighed, still awed by Keisha's oral skills.

He could hear her brushing her teeth as he wondered idly if Ricky had gotten lucky with that sweet young filly.

Keisha exited the bathroom and went out to the kitchen, returning to the bedroom with two bottles of beer. Duane accepted it gratefully, downing half the contents in one swig.

"Wow, somebody was thirsty," Keisha teased, as she took a drink.

"Getting ready for round two," Duane said, massaging her thigh. Keisha opened her legs so he could play with her clean-shaven pussy. Duane cupped it, marveling at the abundance of flesh. He flicked his thumb over her engorged clit and she trembled. He inserted one, then two fingers inside her. Keisha moaned and moved her hips slowly, grinding his fingers.

Duane felt his cock stiffen.

"Fuck me now D," Keisha commanded. "Handle mi like yuh drag racing."

Duane put the beer down and went to put on a condom.

Keisha slipped a finger in her pussy and tasted herself. Duane rolled on the condom in a hurry. Keisha swung her legs onto his shoulders and Duane plunged his dick inside her.

"Yes D, drive me like a stick shift," Keisha breathed. "Make me cum D, juice my fat pussy."

Duane's cock grew bigger inside her as she talked dirty to him. Her tight pussy choked his dick and he struggled not to cum prematurely.

Duane flipped her over and she quickly got on her hands and knees. Her incredible ass seemed to envelope him as he entered her from behind.

"Fuck me hard D," she begged, backing her ass up against his dick, meeting his thrusts.

Duane grunted like a pig, smacking her ass as he plowed into her mightily. He hoped she would climax soon as he knew he wouldn't be able to hold out much longer. Her pussy was just too tight and sweet.

"Ohhhh, that's it...don't you dare fucking stop!" Keisha shouted. "Just like that!"

Keisha reached down and pinched her clit as she emitted an inhumane cry, her pussy throbbing like crazy as she bathed his dick with her juices.

She climaxed not a moment too soon. Duane slapped her huge ass with all his might as he emptied his seed. Keisha squealed from the force of the slap and Duane collapsed on top of her; completely spent. After a couple seconds, he removed the condom, resting it on the night table.

"Bwoy, Keisha, dat was serious," Duane remarked, gazing at her pretty face, which was sweaty from their coupling.

"Mmmm," Keisha mumbled contentedly.

"I hope mi can see you again," Duane continued, "I think I'm hooked already."

"I like you D, but I have a man. An' he's really jealous and possessive," Keisha replied, adding, "But we'll see it how goes."

After a few minutes, they both fell asleep. About an hour and a half later, the phone rang loudly, startling them. Forgetting he wasn't at his home, and before Keisha could stop him, Duane reached over and answered it.

"Hello."

The Revelation

THE REVELATION

*T*he Jenkins lived in a lovely two-storey house, in the affluent neighbourhood of Cherry Gardens, Kingston. They had been married for eight years and Sophia Jenkins was five years older than her husband, Desmond, a stockbroker.

She was thirty-nine and a bit apprehensive about turning forty. Sophia was marginally attractive and had been steadily gaining weight over the past nine months. She had ballooned to a hundred and eighty pounds. Way too much for her five-foot-five-inch frame.

She had tried dieting and exercise, but nothing seemed to work; and though she could afford it, she refused to have the fat surgically removed.

Desmond, for his part, was in fairly good shape. He didn't have a six pack but he was muscular from working out at the Raging Bulls Gym four times a week and he had also recently taken up tennis. Sophia was suspicious when she had found out that the tennis instructor was a hot, young, curly-haired female.

It was nine o' clock, Monday morning, and Desmond had already left for the office. Sophia was on the phone in the bedroom, talking to the manager of her retail furniture store in Ocho Rios. Sophia owned a chain of them island-wide, seven in total, and that branch always seemed to have the most problems.

She sighed after hanging up the phone. *I'm really going to have to fire Janice*, she thought as she headed for the walk-in closet, *she's not coping at all.* Sophia removed a duffel bag from the bottom of her closet and went over to her queen-size bed.

Sophia rummaged through the bag and took out a small butt-plug, a bottle of lube and the purple vibrator called "the rabbit". She switched it on to check the batteries. It hummed loudly. Satisfied, she shrugged off her robe and lubricated the butt-plug. It was about four inches in length. She pulled one of her ample ass cheeks to the side and inserted the plug easily, sighing with pleasure. Her anus accepted it willingly with a loud plop. Sophia then lay on the bed. The bedroom door was wide open but the helper had instructions not to come upstairs while she was home, unless summoned.

Sophia spread her legs, switched on the rabbit and placed it on her pussy. The rabbit had two parts, a thick shaft for penetration, and a small funny shaped section at the base for clitoral stimulation. Sophia moaned as her pussy began to get moist. When it was sufficiently wet, she adjusted the rabbit and inserted the shaft, positioning it so that the small piece was right on her clit.

She put the control button on high, and gasped with pleasure as the phallus vibrated and twisted in her soaking wet pussy. She felt deliciously filled as she felt her first orgasm of the morning approaching.

Enid, the helper, watched as her boss gyrate her fat waist and mutter incoherently. One morning, two weeks ago, Enid had been dusting the sculpture at the foot of the stairs when she heard Mrs. Jenkins groan as if in pain. She had hesitated, knowing that her boss was strict about her rules, but the groans had gotten louder, and it might be an emergency - the poor woman might be hurt. So Enid had walked cautiously up the stairs calling out, "Mrs. Jenkins, yuh alright ma'am?"

She didn't get a response so she had continued up and got the shock of her thirty-five year old life when she reached the open bedroom door.

Mrs. Jenkins was on her back in the middle of the bed with her eyes closed, groaning loudly and furiously shoving a long, slender, pink instrument in and out of her vagina. Her fat body shook mightily as she convulsed in orgasm. Enid had crept away disgusted, and to her horror, aroused at what she had witnessed. Enid was confused; a good Christian woman such as herself should not be excited by such a depraved scene. Her wet pussy suggested otherwise.

Since then, Enid stayed close by the stairs around nine-thirty in the mornings and pretended to clean as she waited to hear if her employer was making any strange sounds. If she heard something, she would then creep up to the bedroom door and watch Mrs. Jenkins pleasure herself. It happened at least three times a week.

"Woi…ughhhh," Sophia wailed, as she climaxed.

Enid slipped away as Sophia's body shook in ecstasy. Enid's big cotton panties were soaked as she hurried down the stairs. Ever since that first morning when she had discovered Mrs. Jenkins masturbating, her pussy had awakened from the dead. For the first time since Tony, her good for nothing ex-husband, had ran off with a young go-go dancer three years ago, she was feeling an ache between her legs.

She had been married to Tony for four years and thought he was happy until she came home from her regular Sunday night church service on that unforgettable Sunday and didn't see him or his belongings. What she did find, however, was a short, handwritten letter from Tony. It had read:

Dear Enid,

I am leaving you for a go-go dancer dat mi did meet two weeks ago. She know how fi satisfy me in bed and she don't get vex and carry on when mi ask har to suck mi wood. Matter of fact she love fi do it. She also mek mi sex har in any position mi want and she give mi pussy anytime mi want it. Mi tired ah yuh Enid, yuh too boring an' miserable. Yuh ago mek mi ole before time, so mi gone before it too late. Take care of yuself.

Love,
Tony

Enid had been shattered. She swore off men and pretty much her life has since been centered on work and church.

Ah, that was a good one, Sophia thought, as she showered. She felt energized, ready to face the day. Desmond wasn't too interested in having sex these days - at least not with her. He hadn't fucked her in nine days and the time before that; he had stopped in the middle of the act, claiming his head hurt. *Must be my increased weight*, Sophia mused as she dried herself. *Oh well, my toys work just fine.*

Forty minutes later, Sophia was in her BMW X5 heading to the office, when her cell phone rang. It was Dionne, her personal assistant.

"Morning, Mrs. J."

"Morning, Dionne."

"Just calling to remind you to bring down the draft for the new contract."

"Shit! Thanks Dionne, if only you had called five minutes earlier. I'll have to turn back and get it."

Sophia pulled over to the gas station and turned the SUV around.

"Morning Mrs. Jenkins," Hubert, the gardener said, as she alighted from the vehicle.

"Morning, Hubie," Sophia replied, adding, "Please remember to get rid of that wasp nest by the garage."

"Yes ma'am," Hubert muttered. *Mi mussi look like pest controller*, he fumed inwardly.

Sophia entered the house and headed upstairs to retrieve the contract. As she neared the top of the stairs, she paused, wondering what the hell was that sound coming from her bedroom. She walked quietly to the open door and her eyes bulged in shock.

Enid was on the floor with her housedress open and her legs widely spread, plunging Sophia's largest dildo into her fat, hairy pussy. Enid's panties and Sophia's duffel bag were next to her feet.

"Enid!" Sophia shouted.

Enid's eyes flew open in fright, as she froze, holding the dildo in mid-plunge; the exposed half slick with her juices.

No one spoke or moved for what seemed like an eternity.

Then Sophia started to undress.

Consequences

CONSEQUENCES

*O*tis was ecstatic to be returning home to Jamaica. He had been away on farm work in Canada for seven months and he had missed home dearly. Otis Bailey was thirty-two years old and hailed from the small farming community of Willowfield in the parish of St. Thomas.

He had a small plot of land behind the one bedroom board house he shared with his common-law-wife, Elaine, where he grew tomatoes. Otis was known for having the biggest and best tomatoes in Willowfield; he always sold off his stock quickly. He hoped George, the fellow he had left in charge, was taking good care of his crop.

Otis had jumped at the opportunity to go away on the farm work program, hoping to earn enough money so he could install a proper bathroom in his house. He was sick and tired of having to go outside to use the latrine whenever nature called. Even if the money he made wasn't enough to finish it, Otis surmised, it was at least a start.

The taxi sped through the town of Bull Bay and Otis admired a voluptuous woman walking with two children. He couldn't wait to get home and have sex with Elaine. It had been seven long months since he'd had some pussy. Elaine was the sexiest woman in the community, all the men in Willowfield lusted mightily at her shapely body and full, firm breasts.

Bigga, a fat schoolboy, had almost gotten killed because of Elaine's lush, sexy body. Bigga had climbed the tall, East Indian mango tree that overlooked Otis' backyard to spy on Elaine while she bathed. The shower stall was a small, square, roofless, zinc structure.

He had overheard Elaine inform Miss Pearl that she was going to bathe before it got dark and he had dashed over to his cousin's house to climb the tree. His cousin Gary had been the one to notice that they had a clear view of Elaine's "bathroom" from the mango tree.

Bigga had been perched on a thick branch, his short, stubby dick fully erect, when Elaine, wearing only a short T-shirt, emerged from the house and went into the shower stall. Bigga had gasped excitedly when Elaine's lush body came into view. Her plump, hairy mound was the fattest pussy he had ever seen. He had spat in his hand and jerked his dick furiously. When Elaine had put the soapy rag between her legs, Bigga had ejaculated and lost his balance. He had fallen from the tree screaming in terror. He survived the fall but suffered multiple lacerations, a sprained back, a dislocated shoulder, a broken leg and wounded pride. It had been the talk of the community for weeks.

The taxi pulled up at his gate and Otis jumped out smiling a wide grin, exposing the wide space his two missing front teeth had left behind.

"Otis!" Elaine shouted with glee, as she ran from the verandah to greet him.

"Yuh did miss mi?" Otis asked as he hugged her tightly, crushing her generous bosom against his muscular chest.

"Of course!" Elaine enthused, feeling his erection straining through his trousers.

The taxi driver helped Otis carry the bags inside the house and left whistling softly to himself, marveling at Elaine's luscious curves.

Otis closed the door quickly and scooped Elaine in his arms. She was heavy, but Otis was big and strong, and carried her easily into the small bedroom. They undressed hurriedly and tumbled onto the bed.

Otis moaned as he kissed Elaine passionately while massaging her moist pussy through the thick mat of pubic hair. Elaine arched against him, caressing his back and neck. Otis, not bothering with much foreplay, rammed his dick inside her.

He was a big man but his dick did not complement his two hundred and ten pound, six-foot-two inch body. It wasn't exactly small but when they had met three years ago, Elaine had expected it to be much bigger.

"Ughhh…" Otis grunted, fucking her as hard as he could. *She feels different, looser*, Otis thought as he pumped his dick into Elaine furiously, but he dismissed it as probably his being away so long.

Elaine moaned intermittently, wishing he would hurry up and climax so she could see what gifts he had brought back for her.

"Geezam…mi ah cum baby," Otis breathed as he shot a torrid stream of thick semen into Elaine's depths.

"Bwoy, mi did really need dat," Otis remarked contentedly as he lay by her side, trying to catch his breath.

"Me too," Elaine responded appropriately.

After ten minutes of talking and catching up on the happenings in the community, Otis got up and unpacked. Elaine was elated with her gifts. Otis had bought her four pairs of shoes, a couple of summer dresses, six floral blouses and some sexy underwear.

She especially loved the red, lace thong and wondered when she would she get a chance to wear it for Errol.

Elaine had met Errol one month after Otis had left for Canada. He had moved to Willowfield to assist his uncle in running the wholesale shop. His uncle had arthritis and was unable to manage the shop on a day to day basis.

She had gone to the shop to get some groceries one Saturday and they had hit it off immediately. There was just something about him that drove her wild. After that initial first meeting, she went back the following three days, unable to stay away. Willowfield was a small close-knit community so she had to be careful if she didn't want Otis to find out. They made plans to meet down by the river on Sunday evening, when most people were either at church, or gathered under the streetlight playing dominoes.

He was there when she arrived at the clump of bushes behind the huge set of rocks adjacent to the river.

"Yuh early," she had remarked, her body tingling with anticipation. Errol had responded by kissing her roughly with passion, hiking up her skirt. She had moaned with pleasure and rubbed his crotch, gasping excitedly when she felt how big he was. He had promptly dropped his pants to his ankles and pulled down her panties, shaking one of her legs free.

It was difficult for him to enter her at first, despite the fact that her pussy was so wet that her juices were running down her thick thighs. Eventually she had slowly stretched to accommodate him and Errol had to stuff her panties in her mouth to muffle her screams. Elaine had felt sure he was going to break her in two. She had walked home gingerly, feeling like he was still embedded in her. She loved the feeling.

But now Otis was back. She had to come up with a plan to fuck Errol soon. She had gotten hooked on getting a dose of his big wood at least once a week.

"Otis, is Saturday night is Miss Bell nine-night," Elaine remarked, "Yuh going?"

"Yeah man," Otis responded, "She used to be close to mi family."

Miss Bell had passed away in her sleep over a week ago and was to be buried on Sunday.

She was well loved in the community, having lived there for over eighty years. A huge crowd was expected at the nine-night.

Two days later, Thursday, Elaine went down to the wholesale shop under the pretext of buying milk and set a time with Errol to meet at their usual spot on Saturday night, while Otis would be busy mingling with friends and playing dominoes.

Saturday night came and Elaine dressed up in one of her new summer dresses and set off to the nine-night excitedly with Otis, holding hands as they walked the mile or so up to where the nine-night was being held. They could hear the loud singing as they approached.

When they arrived, Otis went straight to the domino table and Elaine went to chat with the group of young women sitting on a bench close to the goat-head soup. At eight, she excused herself and went to check on Otis at the domino table. He was having a good time and he smiled proudly when Elaine kissed him on his lips in front of his friends.

Elaine then drifted through the crowd and hurried down to the river, which was only a quarter mile away. She was so preoccupied she didn't notice the man pissing in the bushes, watching her with a curious look on his face.

"Six love!" Otis yelled triumphantly, as he slammed the winning domino down on the table. "Who nex'?" he asked, beating his chest.

Errol was waiting when she got there.

"Hurry up baby," Elaine implored, as she immediately took off her panties, "We nuh really have much time."

"Alright babes," Errol responded as he sat on the grass.

Elaine positioned her gaping pussy over his rigid cock and lowered herself slowly. She groaned in pain as she took in every inch. The feeling was always the same, her pussy could never get used to a cock of this magnitude but yet she couldn't get enough of it.

"Lawd god..." Elaine cried, as she rode his dick slowly.

George couldn't see them from where he stood but he could definitely hear them. He had been taking a piss when Elaine had rushed pass him. Curious, he had followed her.

"Yuh cocky too big Errol," he heard her say. He was shocked when he heard her call Errol's name. George hated Errol because he wouldn't give him goods on credit when he had no money. *Yuh bugga yuh*, George thought maliciously, as he hurried back to inform Otis of his discovery.

Errol was now fucking Elaine doggy style, he loved to smack her fleshy ass and feel it jiggle as he plunged his huge tool inside her.

"Otis! Otis!" George huffed as he reached the domino table, where Otis was administering his second six love of the evening.

"George, wah wrong wid yuh man?" Otis asked, as everyone around the table stared at George questioningly.

"Otis, mi jus' see Elaine an' Errol dung ah de river ah sex," George stammered, trying to catch his breath.

At first Otis was dumbstruck, as his brain tried to process the disturbing information. The table was silent, everyone shocked in disbelief. A kaleidoscope of emotions played on Otis' face: embarrassment, shame, anguish, anger.

"Go chop up dem bloodclaat Otis!" someone yelled, breaking the silence. Suddenly, Otis jumped into action, knocking over the domino table.

"Somebody gimme a machete!" he screamed, his eyes wild.

Someone from the crowd complied, and Otis grabbed it and took off at high speed down to the river. Word spread quickly around the nine-night, and people rushed after Otis to witness the drama.

"Mi feel like mi want fi pee," Elaine breathed, as Errol fucked her mercilessly.

"Piss then, mi nuh care," Errol declared nastily, not easing up the pressure. Elaine moaned loudly and tightened her grip on the tree trunk.

Otis ran like a track star down to the river, adrenaline pumping through his veins. Not even Flash, who was the champion runner at Willowfield Primary School, could keep pace with him. The sharp machete glistened wickedly in the moonlight as he ran.

Otis reached the river and looked around for the objects of his wrath. He looked like a mad man. His face was shiny and sweaty, and bruised from his grueling run through the bushes. His muscular chest was heaving mightily.

"Tek buddy gal!" was the instruction Otis heard from the direction of the huge set of rocks by the clump of trees and bushes about two hundred meters away.

Otis emitted a guttural roar and took off in the direction of the sound, his eyes red with rage. How could she?

Errol and Elaine screamed simultaneously in absolute terror when Otis charged through the bush with his machete raised.

The Best Man

THE BEST MAN

"We were at the Jamdown Grill and Restaurant, a hip eatery on Hope Road in Kingston. The night was starry and cool, the food spicy and delicious, and I was feeling exuberant. I was getting married in seven days! I'm so happy, I thought, as I gazed into my fiancé's eyes across the small, intimate table.

Bruce had proposed to me three months ago. A delivery guy had brought me flowers and a box, and in the box, had been an engagement ring. My cell phone had rung immediately and Bruce had uttered the four words I always wished I would hear one day "Will you marry me?"

I had whispered yes, and Bruce had stepped into the office, smiling. I had ran to him, hugging him tightly, sobbing, overcome with emotion. My co-workers and boss had cheered; I was too happy to be embarrassed.

"So, Jerome is coming on Friday," Bruce announced, breaking into my thoughts. "I offered to let him stay at my apartment but he's reserved a suite at the Sun San Hotel."

"Ok, it will be good to finally meet him," I responded. Jerome is Bruce's oldest friend; they go way back. Bruce and I have been together for four years and Jerome had migrated to England five years ago, so I've never met him. I've heard a lot about him though, quite the playboy and according to the photos Bruce has, sinfully handsome. I'm glad he doesn't live here; he would be a bad influence on Bruce with his wild, philandering lifestyle.

"You ready babes?" Bruce was asking. "I have another hunger I need to satisfy," he added, smiling mischievously.

"Is that right Mr. Jones?" I purred. "You better get all you can tonight, because that's it until our honeymoon."

Bruce smiled and paid the bill. We left the restaurant holding hands and arrived at my studio apartment in Mona Gardens, some twenty minutes later.

I put on some slow jams and undressed slowly, as Bruce sat on the bed watching me with lust-filled eyes.

I slipped my sexy black dress down my long, toned legs and stood there in my black lace underwear, swaying seductively to the music.

Bruce moaned in appreciation and took off his shirt. I unhooked my bra and freed my perky breasts. I then turned around and took off my panties, bending over; exposing my juicy pussy to Bruce's piercing eyes.

He groaned at the visual and shrugged off his jeans. I turned and walked over to Bruce, licking my lips seductively. He stood up and took me lovingly in his arms, his stiff dick making a tent of his boxers. I kissed him deeply and reached for his dick through the slit in the front.

I nibbled on his chest as I slowly ran my soft hands up and down his pulsing, rigid shaft.

Bruce gently pushed me to the bed and removed his boxers. He climbed on top of me and took my left breast in his mouth as he entered me slowly. I moaned and wrapped my legs around him, pulling him deeper inside me. Sex with Bruce was always slow and tender. Sometimes I wish he would just ram his dick inside me and fuck me hard; and stop treating me like I was glass or a fine piece of china. That was the only fault I found with Bruce; but how do you tell the man you love that he's boring in bed?

"Oh Mel, I love you so much," Bruce breathed in my ear, as he moved his waist in a slow, circular motion.

"I love you too baby," I replied. And I did; Bruce was a really sweet guy.

Bruce quickened his pace slightly as he neared orgasm. *No, no, not yet!* I screamed inwardly as Bruce squeezed me tightly, shuddering.

"Did you cum baby?" Bruce asked naively, looking down at me with love in his eyes.

"Yes babes," I responded sweetly. *Ah boy, I was just getting warmed up.*

Bruce got up and went to the bathroom to pee and I turned off the CD player and switched on the television, trying to ignore the ache between my legs. We watched a comedy and then Bruce left to go to his apartment.

The week sped by quickly as I finalized the preparations for the wedding. Luckily my best friend Joan and my mom were right by my side, providing much needed support.

My dress was gorgeous and I couldn't wait to wear it down the aisle. It was going to be a small intimate wedding, just close friends and close family members from both sides; forty guests in all. Bruce and I are going to spend our honeymoon at an all-inclusive resort in Negril. I took two weeks vacation, starting Monday, though the honeymoon will only be for a week.

"Oh mi likkle baby gettin' married," my mom said teary-eyed, hugging me tightly. We were at my apartment, packing most of my stuff. On Monday, when I'm in Negril, Joan will organize the removal of my things.

"Its ok mom," I said, crying too. "I'll always be your baby."

My mom and I are very close. My dad lives in Philadelphia and is estranged from the family. I haven't spoken to him in over nine years.

"Mi soon turn grandmother," my mom said, smiling through her tears, as the phone rang.

"How many grandkids you want? Seven?" I teased, getting up to answer the phone.

It was Bruce.

"Hey babes, just coming from the airport," he informed me. "I'm on my way to drop Jerome off at the hotel. He says hi."

"Tell him hi for me."

"We're going out to have drinks at eight babes, so be ready around seven-thirty."

"Ok baby, later."

"Love you."

"Love you too."

Jerome was feeling great. He hadn't realized how much he missed Jamaica until he had stepped out of the airport into the brilliant sunshine, a porter wheeling his Louis Vuitton luggage in tow. It was good to see Bruce; though they were complete opposites, their friendship had stood the test of time.

"You ready for the big day?" Jerome asked, as he lit a cigarette.

"Yeah man!" Bruce enthused, his face lighting up. "Melissa is definitely the woman I want to spend the rest of my life with."

"That's good," Jerome said, "I'll take that step in another twenty years."

They chuckled and Bruce pulled his Honda Accord to a stop in front of the swanky hotel.

"I'll pick you up at eight," Bruce told him as a porter removed Jerome's luggage from the trunk.

"Ok mate, see you later then," Jerome replied.

Jerome swaggered into the hotel lobby and checked in, flirting with the pretty receptionist who was awed by the handsome, charming, well-dressed guest.

Later that night, at five minutes past eight, Bruce and I were seated in the lobby waiting for Jerome to come down. At eight-fifteen, Bruce asked the receptionist to buzz him again.

"He's on his way down now sir," the receptionist informed him.

A minute later, Jerome sauntered in the lobby, fashionably dressed in a grey Armani blazer over jeans and designer trainers.

"Sorry I'm late mate," he apologized, smiling, "had a bit of a nap."

"It's cool," Bruce replied. "This is my darling wife to be, Melissa."

I felt unsteady as I rose to greet him; his presence was overwhelming.

His pictures didn't do him justice. The man was an Adonis.

"Hi gorgeous," he said, giving me a light hug and a peck on the cheek.

"So you're the woman that has my mate running to the altar," he teased.

I smiled nervously. "Nice to finally meet you," I managed.

I walked to the car on rubbery legs, half listening to their light banter as I wondered why the hell my body was still tingling from Jerome's brief touch. We saw Lorraine, Bruce's sister and one of my bridesmaids, out in the parking lot. Her pilot boyfriend was staying at the hotel for two days.

We went to a trendy sports bar on Kingston's hip strip and Jerome ordered a bottle of Hypnotiq to go along with the spicy barbecue wings. Bruce chattered on, oblivious to the electrifying connection between his best friend and I.

I felt confused and ashamed at the insane attraction I was feeling towards him. I'm getting married the day after tomorrow for Christ sakes! I watched as he flirted with the cute waitress, inexplicably feeling jealous when she slipped him her number on a napkin. God he was smooth.

Bruce excused himself to go to the bathroom and I almost got up as well, afraid to be alone with Jerome.

The sexual tension around the table was palpable. We gazed at each other, not speaking. It was as if we were the only two people in the crowded sports bar.

My nipples were as hard as rocks and my pussy was threatening to jump out of my jeans. I was a bitch in absolute heat.

"My room number is 405," he said confidently, looking deeply in my eyes.

The cocky bastard! I thought. Bruce's return saved me from responding to his bold statement.

The rest of the evening was a blur. We left the sports bar an hour later, Bruce half-drunk as he was not used to drinking so much. I drove; stealing glances at Jerome, slouching sexily on the back seat.

He bade us goodnight when we arrived at the hotel, giving me a piercing look as he turned and entered the lobby.

I drove to Bruce's apartment and put him bed where he promptly fell asleep. I sat on the bed, listening to my future husband snore lightly; my mind churning. There is no way I'm fucking my fiancé's best friend two days before our wedding, I sternly told myself as I got up to go home.

I took a shower as soon as I got to my apartment, hoping it would cool me down.

It didn't work.

All I could think about was running my hands and lips all over Jerome's athletic frame, kept wondering if his cock was big, sure that he would fuck me the way I needed to be fucked…oh, I'm going crazy!

I lay on the bed naked with the lights off, knowing I was fighting a losing battle. Thirty minutes later, I was in the hotel lobby.

"Please buzz room 405," I told the receptionist nervously.

"He said to send you right up," he responded, a little smirk playing at the corners of his mouth.

My feet were heavy as I got in the elevator. My heartbeat sounded loud to my ears. My pussy was wetter than I could ever remember it being.

I stood in front of his room door for two minutes before knocking.

He opened the door and stood there in a terrycloth robe, open at the chest, partially showing a huge colourful tattoo. I placed my hand on the door jam for support; I felt weak. Silent, he held out a manicured hand to me, I took it and entered the suite; a lamb to the slaughter.

Neither of us spoke as he crushed his mouth to mine, his tongue darting in my mouth; searching, twirling. I moaned passionately as I shrugged off his robe. He was naked underneath. I gasped with delight as my hands found his thick, heavy dick. I couldn't wait to feel it inside me.

Jerome stepped out of the robe and took off my blouse quickly, throwing it behind him. I groaned loudly as he turned me around and nibbled on the back of my neck while unbuckling my shorts. My body quivered under his touch.

I stepped out of my shorts and he bent me over, smacked my ass and roughly spread my legs. I thought I would faint from excitement.

I braced against the wall as I heard him rip the condom wrapper. I turned my head slightly and looked at him as he rolled the ribbed condom onto his impressive dick.

I screamed with an equal mixture of pain and pleasure when he rammed his dick into my pussy with a powerful thrust. He didn't move for several seconds. My pussy throbbed as it adjusted to his girth.

Then he started to move. I spread my legs wider as he fucked me with long, hard strokes.

"Ohhh...fuck me Jerome," I begged, loving the way he dick filled my pussy to the brim. He was hitting spots and reaching places I didn't know existed.

Jerome smacked my ass repeatedly as he plunged into me rapidly, his testicles slapping against me noisily.

"Good god...I'm coming," I announced as the unfamiliar rush of an orgasm from penetration shook my body like a tsunami. "Ohhhh..." I cried as my juices ran freely down my slender thighs.

Jerome pulled out of my pussy with a loud plop, and I crumbled to the floor. He moved over to the couch and sat there, waiting for me to join him; his majestic dick proudly pointing at the ceiling. I crawled over to him and began to lick his huge testicles. I concentrated on the area between his balls and his anus and elicited the first audible groan from him.

"Ummm...ughh..." Jerome groaned as he ran his hands through my hair. Going off instinct and extremely turned on by his reaction, I pulled him towards me, held his legs in the air and flicked my tongue back and forth over his ass. He moaned loudly and pushed me away as he struggled to regain his composure. He stood and I climbed in his arms, putting my legs around his waist as his dick nudged the entrance of my pussy. He brought me down hard, his dick impaling me like a mighty sword. I screamed with pleasure as I felt it in my belly.

It should be a crime for one man's dick to be so sweet, I thought, as he stood there impaling me with all his might. He spun around and threw me on the couch, still deeply embedded inside me. Sweat poured off his face despite the air conditioning as he fucked me with my feet on his shoulders. I whimpered as I felt my second orgasm approaching.

"Yes, yessssss..." I moaned as I convulsed, overcome by the intensity of it all. Jerome's stamina was incredible. He pulled out and I got on top of him, riding his dick like I was trying to break it off. Jerome grunted as he smacked my ass loudly. He held my ass in mid-air and began thrusting upwards rapidly, muttering incoherently as he finally climaxed. I rolled off him, tired and sweaty, as he got up and went to the bathroom.

I lay there catching my breath, feeling badly about having betrayed Bruce, but honestly not regretting it. That was the simply the most amazing sex I've ever had in all my twenty-eight years. I heard the shower go on and I got up gingerly to join Jerome in the bathroom.

He was soapy, and I rinsed off his flaccid dick and squatted in front of him. The hot water felt wonderful as it cascaded down my back, as I slowly sucked his dick. Amazingly, considering he just fucked the hell out of me for over an hour, he immediately got rock hard. I cupped his balls as I valiantly tried to deep throat his fat dick.

He moaned appreciatively, bracing his hands on the shower wall as he slowly fucked my mouth. I pumped his dick furiously, sucking him with loud slurping noises, gobbling his cock with wild abandon, determined to milk him dry with my mouth.

I laboured for over ten minutes, my mouth growing tired. Almost ready to give up, I felt his balls begin to tighten. I sucked him with renewed vigor as I went for the prize. Jerome's knees buckled as he rewarded me with a heavy load of hot semen in my mouth. I drank it thirstily.

Ten minutes later, we lay on the huge bed; neither of us had said a word since I arrived at his room almost two hours ago.

"I knew you'd come," he finally said, as he puffed on a cigarette.

"I had to," I replied.

Incredibly, he put out the cigarette and reached for me. *Jerome must be an alien* I mused.

I woke up the next morning in a panic at nine o' clock. Shit! What if Bruce called the house already? I got up and quickly got dressed. Jerome walked me to the door, his limp dick swinging like a golf club, and gave me a long, lingering kiss that made me briefly contemplate fucking him one more time before I left.

"Oh Jerome, I have to go," I said reluctantly and opened the door.

My heart did a somersault in my chest as I turned to go down the hallway to the elevator. Looking at me, her mouth and eyes wide open in shock and I assume, disgust, was Lorraine, Bruce's sister and one of my bridesmaids. I had completely forgotten that she was staying at the hotel with her pilot boyfriend for two days.

Mr. Right

MR. RIGHT

"*Where* yuh think yuh goin' to put that?" Janet asked fearfully, as she slowly backed away from Trevor. She appreciated a well-hung man as much as the next girl, but this was ridiculous. Trevor possessed the kind of dick you saw in pictures on the internet and dismissed as being too big to be real.

Trevor just stood there, watching her, knowing that curiosity will soon get the better of her. She would definitely try it out; after all a twelve inch dick wasn't something a woman saw everyday.

Janet bit her quivering lips involuntarily, her big brown eyes rooted at his genitals. *It looks so heavy*, she thought as she squeezed her nipples, unaware that she was doing so. Despite her initial fear, her pussy was getting wetter by the second, excited at the prospect of being penetrated by Trevor's horse dick.

"Come here," Trevor commanded, his anaconda pointing at her menacingly. Janet's feet seemed to move by its own accord as she approached Trevor. She felt like a prisoner on death row taking that last walk to the electric chair. *What have I gotten myself into dear Lord*, she asked herself as she reached out and touched him. It was rock hard. Janet gasped as she held it with both hands, marveling at its weight. Breathing heavily, Janet reached down and cupped his scrotum while she gently stroked his pulsing phallus. His balls were like small grapefruits. *He's truly blessed,* she mused.

Trevor raised her chin and kissed her gently, trying to get her taut, tension-filled body to relax. She responded to his soft kiss, sliding her tongue deeply into his mouth. Trevor sucked on her bottom lip and she moaned in his mouth, her petite hand now stroking his mammoth dick with urgency.

Still kissing her, Trevor moved them over to the edge of the bed and gently pushed her. Janet fell back on the bed and propped herself up by her elbows, wanting to see when he actually penetrated her. But Trevor wasn't ready yet.

She watched in wide-eyed surprise as he got on his knees and began to lick the inside of her thighs. Trevor was the eleventh guy that she was sleeping with and only the second one to go down on her. Extremely aroused at the unexpected bonus, Janet opened her legs wider and swung them back, holding them by the ankles.

Her pussy was now rudely exposed to Trevor's probing tongue. Janet groaned his name as he delicately licked the folds of her pussy, ignoring her throbbing clit for the time being.

"Jesus Christ..." Janet blasphemed softly, as Trevor stuck his tongue inside her as deep as it could possibly go; his hot breath blowing tantalizingly on her engorged clit.

"Ohhhhh..." Janet moaned as he tongue-fucked her rapidly. She placed her legs on his shoulders, unable to hold them back any longer.

Janet grunted with pleasure as Trevor turned his attention to her clit, giving it the softest of licks, teasing her quivering body to orgasm. She grabbed his bald head as he grazed her clit with his teeth, then pursing his lips and sucking it insistently. Janet thrashed under his mouth as she screamed in ecstasy, holding his head firmly in place.

Janet clamped her thighs tightly around Trevor's head as she flooded his mouth with her juices. "Oh my god..." she whispered as she trembled, reeling from the intensity of her orgasm.

Trevor rose, his mouth shiny with her juices and rolled on a condom. Janet was still wary of its size, but feeling more than ready to tackle it. Her pussy pulsed in anticipation as Trevor positioned himself and eased his dick inside her. Janet emitted a piercing cry when he pushed it in to the hilt. She held on to his hips, trying to force him back a bit. Her pussy felt like it was split in two. Trevor removed her hands from his hips and pinned them down on the bed, as he moved slowly but firmly inside her.

"Bloodclaat Trevor, yuh ah go kill mi?" Janet wailed as Trevor increased his tempo. Janet farted loudly, her body succumbing to the intense pressure Trevor was applying to her mid-section.

Trevor didn't stop or comment on the fart, and she was in too much pain to be embarrassed.

"Duh Trevor, hurry up an' cum," Janet begged as he plunged his well-endowed dick powerfully inside her, stretching her pussy to capacity.

"Ughh...Ughhh," Trevor grunted loudly as he finally ejaculated, much to Janet's relief.

Trevor withdrew and removed the condom, breathing heavily. "Mi can't manage yuh Trevor," Janet breathed, her crotch on fire.

"Yuh soon cool down babes," Trevor said soothingly. "Yuh will get use to it soon," he added, smiling.

"Yeah right," Janet said with sarcasm, as she gingerly touched her pussy, checking to see if it was still in one piece.

"Mi haffi mek a move babes," Trevor announced, checking his watch. "I have something to take care of."

"At this time of the night? Stay with mi nuh," Janet implored, looking at him through sleepy, half-open eyes.

"It's important baby," Trevor told her as he got dressed. "I'll buzz you tomorrow."

Janet fell asleep promptly when Trevor left. She was completely worn out.

The following day, Tisha, Janet's best friend, had a good laugh at her expense as Janet recounted the night's activities during lunch at a fast food restaurant. "Mi like him but de bwoy buddy too big," Janet confessed as Tisha shook with laughter. "Girl, mi nearly piss up miself when him tek off him pants."

"Take a picture of it with your camera phone," Tisha said. "I want to see the buddy that make you cut a fart!"

Janet blushed as they both convulsed with laughter. The two friends finished lunch and went back to work. Tisha worked as a receptionist at a real estate firm and Janet was a graphic designer at one of Montego Bay's leading advertising agencies.

Janet had met Trevor in the take-out line at a popular seafood restaurant roughly three and a half weeks ago. He had struck up a conversation with her as she waited in line for her escoveitch fish and she had found him funny and okay looking, if not cute. They had exchanged numbers and Trevor had taken her to the movies the following Saturday night. She had a wonderful time but had gently told him no when he asked to spend the night. She had a strict three week policy; absolutely no pussy until at least three weeks of dating.

Later that night, Janet called Trevor to check if he was okay, as she hadn't heard from him since he left her apartment at two in the morning. His cell phone rang without an answer. *Wonder if he's marrie*d, Janet mused, finding it strange that he didn't have a home phone. Janet switched on the television and turned to a movie. Tisha called her to gossip and Janet fell asleep an hour later, dreaming of Trevor's hurricane tongue and oversized dick.

Five days had now passed since she slept with Trevor and he still hadn't called. Janet was furious, thinking that because he had gotten a 'piece', he had moved on. *Fucking big wood punk*, Janet fumed as she drove along Barnett Street, heading home. *If only I knew where the John crow lived* Janet thought, *I'd go over there and give him a piece of my mind.*

She tried to convince herself that she didn't really care, but she did. Trevor's ability to make her laugh coupled with his fascinating dick and willingness to eat her pussy, made him a prime candidate for a possible long term relationship.

Janet was reading a novel about eleven o' clock that night when the phone rang.

"Hello?"

"Hi babes, it's me."

"What yuh want Trevor?" Janet asked coldly, effectively masking the fact that she was thrilled to hear his voice.

"Ah know you upset," Trevor began, "but my brother died suddenly and I had to go up to Anchovy."

"Oh my god, Trevor I'm so sorry to hear!" Janet gushed, feeling terrible. "Why you didn't call me baby?"

"My cell phone wasn't getting good reception up there babes. Yuh done know say is pure bush up deh so," Trevor replied.

"Ok babes, yuh coming over?" Janet asked hopefully, wanting to hold and comfort him in his time of grief.

"I'm really tired babes," Trevor said, "but cook some nice dinner for me tomorrow and I'll come by around eight and spend the night."

"Ok baby, what yuh want to eat?" Janet asked brightly, now in high spirits.

"Umm, cook oxtail an' beans," Trevor told her, "so see you tomorrow babes."

"Alright baby, bye," Janet replied, as she hung up. *I didn't know he had a brother*, she thought as she got up to see if the oxtail she had in the freezer was enough. *But then, I don't really know much about him. We're going to have a long talk tomorrow*, Janet decided.

The next day, Janet left work promptly at five. She stopped by the supermarket to pick up a few items and hurried home to prepare dinner for Trevor.

She finished cooking at fifteen minutes to eight and hurried to take a shower. After a quick shower, she put on her white lingerie and set the table. Janet was a good cook, her mom had seen to that. The food looked and smelled delicious. She had prepared oxtail & beans, creamy mashed potatoes and white rice. She would give Trevor a choice of either carrot or sour sop juice to wash it down with.

At eight o' clock, Janet covered the food on the table and went over to the couch to watch the television. She surfed through the channels and settled on the local news. The news was back after a commercial break and Janet reached for the phone to call Trevor to let him know his delicious dinner was getting cold.

She froze after dialing the first four digits. Plastered on the television screen was a picture of Trevor. She quickly turned up the volume, *"the CCN reports that at seven-forty five this evening, this man, identified as Trevor Coore, opened fire on the police when he was signaled to stop during a routine spot check on Barnett Street. The police returned fire and Coore was hit twice. He is currently in stable but serious condition at the*

Montego Bay Regional Hospital under heavy police guard. Coore was wanted by the police for his alleged role in the brutal triple murder in Kingston last December..."

Janet fainted.

An excerpt from K. Sean Harris'

BLOOD OF ANGELS II

Chapter 1

The doctor breathed a sigh of relief when the baby finally decided, after twelve hours of labour, to exit its mother's womb. His relief turned to horror when he felt two feet instead of a head. The baby was coming out feet first. A breech birth yet the baby had fully turned in the womb. He had never seen anything like this before.

He almost panicked. Breech babies were usually delivered by C-section as there was a high risk of it getting stuck in the birth canal and suffering brain damage from oxygen deprivation if delivered vaginally. The couple was obviously wealthy. If this ended badly he could get into a lot of trouble. His mind ran amok with the possibilities. Criminal charges for negligence. Losing his license. His life ruined.

Oh mon dieu non! Aidez-moi s'il vous plait!

His hands trembled as the mother, with a triumphant scream, finished pushing out the baby. He quickly cut the umbilical cord, and one of the two nurses attended to the mother as she delivered the afterbirth. He anxiously evaluated the baby, doing a routine test that measured the baby's responsiveness and vital signs.

There was a peal of thunder and a flash of lightning, so bright that its silhouette imprinted on the thick, closed drapes. One of the nurses gasped out loud. A strange hush came over the room.

All eyes were on the baby.

He was not crying.

He appeared to be smiling.

The doctor felt a chill.

Laku took the baby.

Mon beau prince. Vous serez un dieu parmi les homes.

The baby appeared to smile wider in agreement.

Dr. Halloran was unsettled. A quick glance at the two nurses confirmed that they too, were ill at ease. He had been a doctor for sixteen years, and this was the strangest experience that he had ever had. It had been a long and difficult labour, and the father had remained by the woman's side the entire time, silently holding her hand, remaining calm throughout. Then there was the actual birth. The baby had turned around in its mother's womb and came out feet first. Even though he had witnessed it, he could scarcely believe it. The baby's body temperature was erratic though all his vital signs were fine. In fact, he appeared to be in the best possible health. He also had a strange look in his disturbingly beautiful eyes. He seemed aware and focused. It was frightening. And he knew that it wasn't his imagination.

It occurred to him that he had just delivered the anti-Christ.

Ridicules!

Ridiculous or not, the thought took hold and would not go away.

Vous serez un dieu parmi les homes. You will be a god among men, the father had said. Who says that to a newborn baby? The father had paid him and the nurses a tidy sum to deliver the baby at home instead of at the hospital. As far as he was concerned it was money well earned. Tonight was one for the history books.

He watched as the baby, freshly scrubbed and wrapped in a Vuitton blanket, was handed to the mother. She was weak and exhausted, but her eyes were alive and luminous with joy.

"Anpu, my baby. My son...you gave mama hell but it was all worth it," she said, as she cradled him in her arms.

The more he observed the baby, the more he was convinced that something was amiss.

This was not a normal child.

He remembered the sudden and brief bout of thunder and lightning.

Dr. Halloran uttered a prayer inwardly and made the sign of the cross. He had not been to church in awhile but he was definitely going to Mass this Sunday. He needed God's blessings to remove the stain the night's events had left on his consciousness.

The woman had lost a lot of blood and needed medical attention, but his job was done. He was leaving. He simply could not stay here a moment longer. Something was not right in this house.

The father turned and looked at him contemptuously as though he had spoken out loud. Fear, the likes of which he had never felt before, held him in a vice grip. His bowels threatened to embarrass him.

"*Nous irons maintenant,*" Dr. Halloran said nervously, looking away from the man's hypnotic red eyes as he gestured to the nurses to gather their things.

"*Oui, vous devez etre fatigue. Je vais vous sortez,*" Laku responded. "*Merci.*"

Laku kissed Anpu and Chasity on their foreheads, and led the doctor and his nurses out to the foyer.

Laku stared at them intently as they waited for him to open the front door. The three of them experienced a sharp pain in their heads that was so brief it was as though they had imagined it. They walked out to the doctor's van and got in, wondering why they had made a house call to this lovely home.

They had no recollection of anything that had transpired.